A Sentence to Death

A. Carys

A. Carys

The characters and events portrayed in this book are fictitious. Any similarity to real persons, living or dead, is coincidental and not intended by the author.

No part of this book may be reproduced, or stored in a retrieval system, or transmitted in any form or by any means, electronic, mechanical, photocopying, recording, or otherwise, without express written permission of the publisher.

Copyright © 2024 A. Carys

All rights reserved.

BOOKS IN THIS SERIES

Of Doors and Betrayal

The Pickpocket and the Princess

The Master, My Wings, Our Service

'Cos This Is How Villains Are Made

A Circus of Wonder

A Sentence to Death

A Deal With The Devil

Let Her Go

The Three

Queen Rory, The Banished

A. Carys

A Sentence to Death

DEDICATION

I fear today's train driver is in a bad mood, the train has never shaken so violently.

A. Carys

CHAPTER ONE

Sending people off to other countries is my job.

I do it all the time, and I prefer to keep my working relationships professional. But that doesn't happen with Ilana Kiri'gin, esteemed daughter of General Phillip Kiri'gin and Captain James Kiri'gin. Ilana and I are old friends, childhood friends even. We went to the same schools for basic education before attending the same training academy. We graduated with high grades and went straight into work. She's a field agent and myself an Agent Handler; and by sheer chance, *her* Agent Handler. I send her off on assignments both here, in Corvian, and overseas.

Today, I'm preparing to send her to Tibori, a war-torn country in the midst of yet another civil war. The country has always struggled with power. One leader is too harsh, one is too soft, and this has left the country at a permanent imbalance. Ilana's job will involve monitoring the civilians and gathering information that will help us paint a better picture of the Tibori's long term chances of remaining independent. Sooner or later, Tibori will be looking to have help, and the moment they need it, Corvian wants to be ready to swoop in.

Her assignment will last three years, and despite my best efforts not to have her be the assigned agent, I failed. Ilana wants to take on a series of short-term assignments, to be closer to her family for a while her brother Sohan works through his separation anxiety, but our Captain had other ideas and I now have to tell her she'll be gone for three years.

"So, where am I going this time?" Ilana asks as she takes a seat on the corner of my desk.

"Tibori. The Aboa Province. It's filled with uprising rebel leaders, troubled citizens and scared bystanders."

She nods and picks up the file that I slide over to her.

"What am I going to be doing?"

"The usual. Watching, listening, recruiting. Guess how long?"

"One and a half."

I shake my head. "Try again."

She frowns. "Two and half?"

"Nope."

"Three?"

I nod. "Three years."

She groans. "I told Andres that I didn't want anything lengthy. Sohan is having a hard time, and I can't be gone for that long."

"I know, I know. I took your name out of the applications folder as soon as it hit my desk. Seems he was going to choose you anyway. I reminded him about your request when he dropped off the file, but he said he wasn't here to make people happy. Luckily, I got him to agree to give you scheduled radio calls every Friday."

She nods, smiling. "Thanks Jake. Sohan will be ecstatic."

"No problem. We're meeting Andres at four tomorrow morning, don't forget."

She nods. "Anything notable to pack?"

"Nope. Just what you'd take on any recon, civilian clothes being highly recommended."

"You're the best," she says, taking the other files from my hand before walking out of the tent.

I continue working until well after midnight. I didn't even have a lot to do in the grand scheme of things. I make sure to keep on top of the work I'm given, but the small, hill-like stack of files on my desk keeps says otherwise. I've been avoiding going through them for as long as possible, but just looking at them makes me anxious, so before I head to the home tent, I sort through them. It only takes fifteen minutes, and it turns out a lot of them weren't actually for me, so once I've sorted them, I place them on the correct desks.

"J?" a voice from behind me calls. I turn and see Thea.

"T, why aren't you in bed?"

Thea is my partner. We haven't put an official title on it because relationships between serving members, specifically field agents, aren't advised. But with our relationship, it's a grey area. Neither of us work in the field. I'm always here, in camp, receiving and sending off spies and operatives, while Thea works in message decoding and information sorting.

Thea is smart, naturally so. At the Academy, she seemed to absorb the course content just by looking at it. She always scored top of the class in exams with near perfect scores. She tutored me for our finances and tactics classes because I struggled with the theory content. We worked together in the final year heist as well. We didn't win, but it was a great challenge to be a part of. That's where we formed our initial friendship, which later on turned into the relationship that we have now.

"You said you'd be back early tonight. I was worried when you weren't in the tent, I thought maybe you might be stressing out about assignments again."

I shake my head with a smile as I approach her. "I'm fine. Ilana's full assignment file came in late and going over the details is tedious. Then I did some filing, and I was just about to pack up and leave."

"Were you?" she asks as she crosses her arms.

"Yes, I swear."

She sighs. "Okay. Let's go, we're the last ones still out of the tent."

"Yes boss," I mutter playfully as I take hold of her hand and follow her back to our tent. It's a decent sized tent, it should be considering there's six of us sharing it. The camp takes on the classes from the Academy, and a lot of the time they get placed in the same tent. Thea and I share with our old classmates Rydell, Sean, Alex and Ilana.

We walk into the tent, being careful to not make too much noise since the others are already tucked up under their blankets. I quickly change into my night clothes before settling down in my cot. Thea's is right next to mine; we actually moved them closer so that we were nearly sleeping on a double cot. As soon as she gets under her blanket, Thea closes her eyes and almost instantly drifts off to sleep.

I, on the other hand, struggle to even get close to sleep. I toss and turn and watch the hands on my watch tick through the hours. I can't sleep. My mind is working a million miles an hour and a feeling that I can't quite describe is eating away at my nerves.

I continue to toss and turn until Ilana gets out of

bed at half three. She wanders over to the shower curtain and pulls it across. I listen to the shower start before rolling out of my cot and changing into a clean set of work wear. A white shirt, black trousers and a thin jacket with our names and ranks embroidered onto it. I run a thin comb through my hair before grabbing my bag and heading over to my work tent.

I grab a few files that need to be read over and shove them into my bag. I then dig around in the bottom draw of my desk, grabbing a snack bar before filling up my water canteen. Then I head to Captain Andres' tent to wait for Ilana.

"Good morning," Ilana says as she arrives not even a few minutes later with Captain Andres hot on her heels.

"Morning," I greet as we follow Andres inside. We all sit down, Ilana and I on one side of the desk, Andres on the other.

"Ilana, I know you've been after short term assignments, but I don't trust anyone else with this particular job. It's sensitive, and the people I need you to recruit are jumpy and distrusting. You are the best one for this job and I wouldn't have put you forward if I had anyone else."

"Yes, Sir."

"I'm sure Jake has filled you in on the rest of your assignment."

"He has. I have the files and I'll read them on the way to the docks."

"Good. Jake, are you okay to escort Ilana to the docks?"

"Of course, Sir."

"Good. The carriage will meet you outside the grounds. Good luck, and make sure to stay in contact."

Ilana and I say goodbye to Captain Andres before heading toward the edge of the campgrounds. Just as we step out of the gate, the carriage pulls up.

"Ilana Kiri'gin and Jake Mills?" the driver asks. We both nod and he gestures for us to get in.

I grab hold of the door handle and pull it open. I offer my hand to Ilana, which she takes with a smile before climbing into the carriage. I follow close behind her and I close the door once I'm seated. The carriage pulls away almost instantly, heading along the track that will take us directly to the docks.

During the journey, we politely ignore each other. I sit and read through dissected agent reports that I'll need to discuss with Captain Andres upon my return, while Ilana reads over her case file. It's a decently thick file containing a new name, address, part time job, back story, identification papers for getting through security checks and a permit for being able to work at the part time job previously mentioned. A lot went into planning this assignment and Ilana gives the file her undivided attention.

My file becomes boring as I keep glancing up at Ilana, and the same bad feeling returns. It crawls up my spine and niggles away at the back of my mind. I shuffle closer to the windowpane in the door. I move the curtain slightly to the side and peer out. Nothing but dead grass and sparse trees for all the eye can see. I let go of the curtain and shuffle to the other side of the carriage before taking a look out the window. Nothing again. We're the only ones on the road, but I can't help the strange feeling I'm getting again.

"Everything alright?" Ilana asks.

"All good."

※

The rest of the ride passes relatively quickly and before I know it we're at the docks. The driver comes round and opens the door for us. I get out first before reaching back in and grabbing my rucksack. I swing one strap over my shoulder before reaching back for Ilana's backpack and duffle bag. I then offer my hand to her as she climbs down the steep steps.

"20 minutes then I'm gone," the driver says grumpily.

"Noted."

"Thank you," Ilana says as we walk over to the departure area.

"You ready?"

"Born ready."

"Here is your new passport and your ticket. There will be someone to collect you on the other side. They'll take you to your residence and they'll also collect biweekly reports from you. Here is a radio tapper as well, this will help you connect onto radio frequencies in your area along with changing to the secure channel to speak with your family," I explain as I hand her everything. She loads everything into her duffel bag before zipping it up.

She nods. "Thank you."

"Anytime. Good luck out there."

She smiles. "I'll see you in three years, I guess."

"See you in three years."

We hug before I watch her disappear into the crowd. I wait to see if she'll wave once she's past the security, and she does. She does a little jump while waving like a maniac. I wave back with a smile before returning to the carriage. It's always sad to see her go, but I know that she'll be fine. She's done this before and I know she can look after herself, but I can't help that nagging feeling that settles at the back of mind.

CHAPTER TWO

The minute I jump out of the carriage, Rydell grabs me by the wrist and drags me to Captain Andres's tent.

"Ry, what's going on?" I ask as I try to lighten her ever tightening grip on my wrist.

"You'll know when we get there."

We burst into the tent, and I'm greeted by a lot of people. Alex, Sean, Thea, Elsie, Rydell, Rune, Sohan, General Phillip, Captain James and Captain Andres.

"What's going on?" I ask as I sit next to Thea.

"We've called you all here because there have been some worrying events sweeping across the country. It's something we're working hard to contain so it's vital it stays between us," Andres says. Everyone nods, silently agreeing to not let the information leave this tent.

"Over the last two weeks," General Phillip begins. "Citizens across the country have been going missing. So far, our reports are suggesting 15 people. Figures we were shown this morning predict that this number will rise significantly over the next few weeks."

"What do you think is happening?" Alex asks.

"We're not entirely sure, but the people who have gone missing all have a common family history. In your classes, you may have been taught about the Pabrian and Bordovan Defectors."

Elsie and I take deep breaths in as we share a glance. Everyone else nods.

"We believe these disappearances are linked to those who defected just over seventy years ago. We believe the people being taken are the descendants, people your age, and slightly older, who the Bordovan spies have managed to identify as relatives of the Defectors," Captain James says as he unveils a board with maps, pins and string drawn all over it.

"Is it possible that they'll come for us?" Elsie asks.

"We don't know. At this point it's a theory because two of the people who have gone missing don't appear to have a *familiar* link to a Defector."

"Do you know for sure that it is Bordova?" I ask.

"We are assuming so. Our outposts around the country have been reporting an influx of what they believe to be Bordovan military agents entering the country. We've started to increase the security at the ports and stricter measures have been brought in when it comes to letting people with work permits and stamps in."

I nod.

"There is still a lot to explore and that will take some time, so we are asking for you eight to take on parts of the investigation. You'll offload your current work and assignments to others around the camp."

Everyone mutters in agreement to taking on this job. Andres passes out papers and pens which he tells us to sign. NDAs. Ensuring that we keep this between us unless we are told otherwise. We hand back the papers and pens before retaking our seats.

"Can someone re-explain the whole Defector history, please?" Sean asks. Andres nods before heading over to the pin board.

CHAPTER THREE

"It's a complicated matter, one that we tried to investigate but couldn't due to a lack of information," Andres starts before handing over to Captain James.

"We still don't have all the information since the Defectors, the ones who ended up in Bordova, all stuck to the same story. They were very careful with how much they told us and how far they were willing to expand on what they said. While we as a military effort don't have all of the information, I believe that Jake and Elsie might be able to give us more of an insight."

Everyone turns to look at Elsie and I. We look at each other, exchanging semi displeased facial expressions before I push up from my chair and walk over to the pin board. Elsie follows and stands there quietly.

"I don't know how much more information I have, but the main part of the story is that Bordova went through a period where they were attacking random camps and locations in countries such as Madoneia and Tibori. There were also rumours that the House was planning some kind of hostile attack on Altaine. Capturing the *Gifted* and then using their power within the Bordovan mutants to try and take over Altaine completely. But the rumours were never confirmed, so the whole story of why the Defectors did what they did is shrouded in misinformation. If you asked a Defector they would tell you one thing, but if you asked the Bordovan's, they'd tell you something completely different."

"One of the other rumours that was going round was that the Defectors were all approached by Pabrian and Corvian spies. They were asked to feed information back to both armies, all while continuing to show their loyalty to the Bordovan army," Elsie says, and everyone nods.

"We both have grandparents who were Defectors, so we are privy to a lot of the finer details. The number of Defectors was roughly two hundred, over a third of them went and sought shelter in Pabria, while the rest made their way here. From there, most of them signed up to the Military and provided all of the information they were willing to give up. Bordova has since been still and unmoving in all military departments."

"But why now? Why start kidnapping the relatives of the Defectors now?" Rune asks.

"Those are good questions. I could only give you a rough answer and that would be that now they deem it the time to punish those who crossed them. There wouldn't be any point punishing the Defectors themselves because most of them are elderly now. That'd be too little justice. The damage is done, they can't change that. Instead, I think that by taking the younger family members, they think they can punish the Defectors through loss and grief," Elsie responds. I nod in agreement.

"Thank you, both of you, for sharing that information," says Commander Phillip as he gathers up manila coloured files from Andres desk. He comes back over and hands the folders out.

"Over the next few weeks, we'll be sending you out in pairs to take statements from the families affected by the disappearances. Then we'll work through correlating the data which will help us put a full picture together. In these files are the dates and areas you're going to be sent too."

We all flick through our folders, nodding in recognition of our assignments.

"You're all dismissed for today. Make sure you keep the orange wires in your desk radios just in case we need to contact you."

A murmur of *yes sirs* filters around the tent as everyone starts to stack their chairs away. We all leave, heading off to sort out the best way to delegate our workloads.

CHAPTER FOUR

My first task in the manila folder is to speak to my family about our history. Specifically, my grandmother as she was a Defector.

After sending a letter to my mother, asking if we could come visit her and my grandmother, we heard back and decided to visit today. Thea and I woke up early, we changed and then grabbed a takeaway breakfast bag before catching a carriage into the heart of Bordova's Main City.

"Hi Ma," I say as I kiss her on the cheek. She was waiting on the doorstep for us and as soon as we stepped out of the carriage she scooped us into her arms.

"*Ey, mi li'tet sakcho*. So good to see you again," she exclaims as she ushers us into the house.

"Thea, it's so good to see you again. *Mia srolto, reba yael mi toullo romazitca ilo Jake arsh dianquo orow pari anniversitaro.*"

"No, no Ma. We need to speak with Grandma about something. It's important."

My mother rolls her eyes but leads us to the conservatory where grandma normally takes her lunch. When we step inside, grandma's eyes light up and she starts speaking Bordovan. She can speak both Bordovan and Corvanese fluently, but whenever she is excited about something, she always speaks Bordovan.

"Hi Grandma."

"*Ey, mi li'tet sakcho.* Let me look at you. My god, you've grown so handsome."

"Thank you," I smile sheepishly at the compliment. "Grandma, we need to talk to you about something."

"What is it?" she asks as she offers us a seat on her bird-watching bench.

"I know you don't like to talk about it a lot, but I need to know more about the Defectors. I need to know more about why you all left."

"Why?"

"People related to Defectors have been going missing. 15 people have gone missing in the last two weeks alone and we've been assigned to a task force. The task force is looking to figure out what is going on, so we can make attempts to prevent more of these disappearances."

She nods and looks out the window, taking a deep breath.

"There is not much to tell, *mi sakcho,* we left for our own safety, but also because we didn't agree with what they were doing. Targeting the *Gifted* and using them for their own personal gain is wrong. We didn't agree with it but there wasn't a lot we could do," she says, still looking out the window.

"What made everyone choose here and Pabria?" Thea asks as she pulls out a notepad and pen.

"We were approached by undercover operatives from both countries. They offered us sanctuary if we could give them all of the information we had on the House. Back then, Captains, Commanders, and many of the higher ups were loose lipped. They didn't care who heard what they were talking about because they seemed to think that everyone was as corrupt as them."

"And once you made your way to Corvian, what were you offered to help keep you from being found?" Thea asks without looking up as she scribbles.

"We were given new names for our personal lives, and new identities for our military service. Our trips over here were covered with military personnel papers and pre-registered identification papers."

"So everything was secure?" I ask this time.

"Everything was secure. There was no way they would've been able to track us."

"And what was your military service in Bordova like?"

"I was in the field a lot of the time. I was part of the team that was sent to look into Altaine and its *Gifted*. We needed to figure out the possible weak links in the country. A few of the *Gifted* that we'd convinced to come back to Bordova with us were taken away. That same night we heard them screaming, crying. They were being tortured for information. I lost a little piece of myself that night and I began to rethink my position in the Bordovan military."

"That was when you decided you didn't want to be a part of that?"

"Yes. I was reluctant to go on more overseas assignments, but I had to keep up appearances. I couldn't just stop."

I squeeze her hand when I notice her bottom lip wobble a little. "When did you find out that the others were feeling the same?"

"A few months after I decided I didn't like what they were doing. I was approached in the dead of night by three people who were already in the group. We met once a week at breakfast to carefully discuss our next moves. It was a few weeks after we all got together that we were approached by the undercover operatives."

"Okay, thank you, Grandma. I know it's not easy to talk about, so we'll leave it at that. I think we can put the rest together."

"You're most welcome *mi sakcho,* I hope you find out who is doing this, but also make sure you are looking out for yourself. Don't let them get you."

"I promise, I'll be careful."

"Good. And make sure you come visit more often, we miss you."

I smile at her and place a kiss on her cheek. "Anything for you grandma."

"And you, Thea, make sure he keeps up the romance. Lord knows he takes after his father when it comes to being romantic."

Thea laughs. "Of course, ma'am. It was lovely to see you again."

After saying goodbye to my parents, and being given sandwiches for the journey back, we begin the second part of the day's task. Knocking on doors of the residents of Shire Street, where not one, but three disappearances took place just last week.

CHAPTER FIVE

Some residents are more than willing to speak to us, others, not so much.

So far we've taken ten statements, had five doors slammed in our faces and three insults thrown at us. But some of the residents are helpful. We've been given descriptions of three strange and definitely out of place looking people who had come around the week before. They'd apparently been scouting out the place and then, all of a sudden, Darrel King, Ellis Aaron and Sara Sparrow were reported missing.

"Thank you, sir, for your help. It's greatly appreciated," I say to the man living at house number nineteen.

"My pleasure, son. Just make sure you bring those kids back in one piece."

"Well try our best sir." I walk down the few steps from his house and meet Thea back on the pavement.

"Break for lunch?" she asks as we walk toward the next house.

"Sure."

We take a seat on the edge of the pavement and pull out the sandwiches my mother gave us. We unwrap the brown paper and eat in relative silence.

"Do you wonder if they'll come for you?" Thea asks randomly.

"What do you mean?"

She places her sandwich down. "The Bordovans. Do you think that they'll come for you?"

I shrug. "They might, there's always going to be that possibility. Somehow, though, I don't think they'll be able to get to me from inside of the camp. The patrols are frequent, and the housing tents are in the middle. It'd be too much effort and I highly doubt Bordova would risk potential political backlash over the kidnappings of official military members."

"But it's possible, right? They could get you on residential visits or when you're out and about with your agents."

"T, I don't want you to think about that. But if it happens, it happens, and if it doesn't then that's great. But if it does, I want you to get into contact with Ilana. She has contacts in Bordova who can help. Tell Andres I told you that and get him to give you her current address in Tibori."

"I will." She leans over and presses a chaste kiss to my lips before moving back and finishing off her sandwich.

After lunch, we continue knocking on doors until it's time to head back to the carriage. As we walk through an empty side street, the sound of many boots on the concrete catches my attention.

"T, do you have a mirror on you?"

She looks at me funny. "Why?"

"I think we're being followed."

"What?" she says with a panicked tone. I gently place a hand on her lower back for comfort as I guide her to walk slightly in front of me.

"Keep your voice down," I say deeply, trying to keep my own voice down, but also trying to portray the seriousness of the situation.

She rummages around in her bag and pulls out a

compact mirror. She opens it and angles it so that she can see behind her.

"We are. Three of them." Panic laces her tone and I resist the urge to pull her into me. Instead, I grab her hand and squeeze it.

"Okay," I say as I take a deep breath. My mind goes into overdrive as I try to think of a plan. "We're two streets away from the carriage pick up and we have thirty minutes until it arrives. If things go wrong, I want you to run and get help."

"No, I'm staying with you."

"Thea, we need to split up and reconvene at the carriage pickup."

"What if they try to take you?"

"Then they take me. Thea, you need to do what I say otherwise this won't end well. You are not field trained in the slightest, and neither am I but that is our best option right now."

She nods, appearing slightly calmer. "Okay. okay, let's do it."

"Good girl," I say as we continue walking. "We're going to turn left at the end of the road and duck into an alleyway or hide behind something.

We'll wait for them to pass and then we'll make our way to the carriage pick up area."

She nods and we follow the plan I just laid out. We turn left and the duck into a shadow covered alley. We wait and watch as a group of three heavily built and tattooed guys pass by. They look around, checking behind the large waste bins and downside streets until they peer into the one we're hiding in. To be honest, this wasn't my smartest plan. We should've continued walking and tried to find a free carriage for an early ride back. But at the same time, it's a plan that should keep us relatively safe. *Relatively alive, even.*

"What's the army doing poking their nose in something that doesn't concern them?" says one of the guys as he comes closer, getting right up in our personal space. I cradle Thea to my chest, her face pressing into my standard issue uniform.

"Based on your accent, I'd say you're the ones in the wrong place. What are three guys like you guys doing wandering around the family residential areas?"

"Just a little business," he says as he pulls Thea out of my grip and pushes her out of the way. He swings at me, his fist catching me in the chin. I stumble but recover quickly and land a punch of my own to the side of his head. He yells and the other two come over and start swinging at me as well.

"Thea, go," I yell. I just manage to catch her running out the alley, but she doesn't get away unnoticed as one of the Bordovans chases after her.

The other two continue their attack. They continue to punch and kick me. I feel one of my ribs crack when one kicks me with his heavy boot. I groan and land on one knee, but I use it to my advantage and sweep out their legs. They both land with a thud and I manage to disable both of them. I root around in my bag and pull out the emergency ties and secure them to the drainpipe.

I limp out of the side street and follow the path I think Thea took. I know I'm right when I see her slouched next to the body of the guy who chased her. He too is tied to the drainpipe.

"You alright?" I ask, kneeling down next to her.

She nods. "He got me good, but I'm fine." She gestures to her freshly busted lip, the cut on her hairline and her left arm that she's cradling to her chest.

"The carriage should be here soon. Let's go before they wake up." I loop my arm under her armpits and help her up. We both limp through the second side street and then down the next main road. The carriage to take us back to camp pulls to a stop as we reach the edge of the pavement.

"You two look rough."

"Just get us back to the camp as quickly as you can. Please," I say to the driver as I open the door to the carriage.

"Sure thing," says the driver, as he grabs the reins from his lap.

We carefully clamber into the back of the carriage. We sit as best we can, groaning at the pain running through our bodies.

"How's your pain?" I ask as the carriage jolts into motion, making us both groan.

"About five. My wrist is the worst."

I nod. "Take off your scarf and use it as a sling," I tell her. Everyone has a standard issue scarf and winter jacket as part of their uniform. Corvian has extremely harsh winters and being in a close proximity to the docks means we receive the worst of the winter winds. But today we only really needed the scarf, the slightly chilly breeze only catching us every now and then. "Tie it and then brace your arm inside it."

She nods and does exactly what I told her to. We sit in silence for the rest of the trip, the only sound coming from either of us are groans of pain as the carriage jostles and bounces its way along the dirt roads.

CHAPTER SIX

"Oh my god."

Rydell bursts into the medical tent with Andres and Captain James following her. She gasps when she sees the state of us.

"What happened?" she asks as she gets closer to Thea.

"Three Bordovan's who were not particularly pleased to find us asking questions," Thea says quietly as the nurse continues to stitch up the wound on her hairline.

"Tried to lose them but they weren't stupid. I took on two while the third chased T. She got a good swing at him and when I found them, he was unconscious."

"Where was the attack?" Captain James asks,

taking out his notepad and pen.

"Shire Street was where I spotted them, but I didn't get the name of the street next to it. It was directly between Shire and the street with the carriage pickups. It should be easily identifiable on a map, or we can take you back and show you," I offer, and the nurse lets me put my shirt back on now that she's finished wrapping and checking my ribs.

Captain James nods. "At some point we'll go back, and you can show us where everything happened. It was three guys, right?"

I nod. "Yes. When we left them, they were tied up, but I'm sure they would've woken up by now and disappeared. We weren't going to hang around and find out what happened next."

"That's understandable. I wouldn't ask you to put yourselves in obvious danger. We'll have someone come and take your full statements before I assign someone else to investigate the incident further."

"Thank you, Sir."

"Just doing my job. I want both of you to take the next few days to rest and recuperate."

We both say thank you, and as both Captains go

to leave, Thea calls out to Andres.

"Sir, what measures will be taken to ensure the safety of the military members who are descendants of the Defectors?"

"We've stepped up the patrols around the gated edge of the camp. Doubled internal patrols that change every four hours so that people are fresh and observant. Over the next few days we're going to be warning groups around the camps of what is going on. Everyone will be told to be vigilant and on guard. We will do all we can to stop the Bordovans from taking anyone else."

Thea nods, letting out a deep breath. "Thank you, Sir."

"No problem. Now get some rest."

Captain James and Andres leave, but Rydell stays and starts fawning over Thea, which freaks her out a little bit. Rydell isn't the cuddly or soft friend of the group. She's the one that scowls and bares her teeth at people she doesn't like. She's like a snake, always coiled and ready to attack. But right now, she's acting like a mother hen as she reassesses Thea's injuries.

"Ry, I'm fine," Thea says as she tries to stand up,

but Rydell is blocking her. "I promise. My arm is in a cast and the nurse said I got lucky with the head wound. Please, stop crowding me."

"You're not fine, T. You're hurt and the nurse didn't just say those things, she also said you might have a cracked rib and a sprained shoulder. May I remind you that a sprained shoulder can lead to—"

"Yes, I know, reduced movement in the shoulder joint and when lifting said arm above the head. Oh, and don't forget the possibility of acute or chronic pain. I did the first aid class as well, and I'm okay for the moment," she says and Rydell pulls a face.

"Thank you for your concern, Ry, it's greatly appreciated. But right now, I would like to go and sit with Jake."

Rydell makes a sound close to a grunt before moving out of the way, letting Thea slide off the bed. I sit up on my bed and scoot back so that I'm supported by the wall. I open my legs and Thea clambers onto the bed, shuffling backwards until her back is resting against my chest.

"This doesn't hurt you, does it?"

"No, sweetheart, it doesn't."

I look up at Rydell just in time to catch her fake gag. "You two make me sick. Enjoy your injuries and I hope you feel better soon," she says with a slight sarcastic tone.

"Bye Ry," Thea says as she rests her head back on my chest.

We sit there for a while, resting and enjoying each other's company. Thea falls asleep before me; steady breaths and light snores fill the medical tent. While she sleeps, I let my mind wander into the mess that has become of the Bordovan Defectors, and I wonder how safe I truly am here in the camp.

CHAPTER SEVEN

Two years and eight months pass by quite quickly, especially when there's a lot to do.

Our wounds have healed nicely, well, except for Thea's shoulder which has ended up leaving her with a small amount of restricted movement when it comes to lifting the arm above her head. Captain Andres referred her to physical therapy to work on loosening the joint and to help alleviate the pain she sometimes experiences.

Other than being in physical therapy, Thea, along with everyone else, has been working hard on the task force. We've made a little bit of progress when it comes to finding out where the citizens who were kidnapped were taken upon landing in Bordova. We think it's somewhere in Farnay, the capital of Bordova, but we're not entirely sure since it's hard to find a pattern in the kidnappings. There isn't a certain type of person they are taking, the familiar relationship doesn't have to be immediate, not in the sense of a first cousin or a nephew. They just have to be a blood relative of the Defector.

The slightly good news is that the disappearances started to taper off about six months ago. While that's the good news, the not so good news is that it has left us with a total of 175 missing people. We'd tried to get people we thought might be targets into hiding, but the number of people who could have been taken was so high that it was hard to prioritise one person over another. So to keep things fair, no one went into hiding provided by the military, but they were given the option to do it themselves if they were truly that scared for their lives.

"How's the board coming along?" Rune asks, gesturing to the board of locations that I've been working on all day.

"It's coming along slowly. There's so many locations they could've been taken to. I'm not sure if we can successfully locate them without having someone actually show us the location."

"Okay. I have an idea," Sean says, jumping up from his chair. "What if we set up a decoy? Someone deliberately asking questions about the disappearances which might draw the attention of whatever spies are still living here. We set them up with radio wires and as soon as they can get hold of a radio in Bordova, they contact us and let us know where they were taken. Boom, solved."

"The only problem with that is if the spies figure out what is going on before they even get out of the country. Bordovan's aren't stupid. They'd know if they were being set up," says Sohan as he pushes Sean back down into his seat.

"Do you have any ideas then, Sohan?"

He shrugs. "No. At least not any smart ones."

Everyone nods. At least he's honest about not having any good ideas.

"The only thing I can think of is that we send scouts. We have someone pretending to be a descendant, maybe someone who looks like they're from Pabria, but they are here asking questions," I suggest, and it seems to catch everyone's attention. "Before that we set up a team to monitor the situation closely and before the person pretending to be a descendant can be taken out of the country, we extract them and imprison the spies who were with them."

"That is a brilliant idea. Write it down and we can take it to the Captains tomorrow," Rune says as he starts packing up his stuff.

I nod and note down my idea before tucking it safely in my desk drawer.

"You coming for drinks tonight?" Alex asks me as he walks past my desk.

"Not tonight. Gonna catch up on some work and then head to bed."

He nods. "Night man."

"Night."

Everyone else leaves, quietly filtering out which leaves me to finish up my work. I move files around and tidy up my desk. I organise everything for tomorrow when a sound outside of the tent catches my attention. The sound happens again, and I try to ignore it as I grab my rucksack and head for the back exit instead.

I check either side of the tent before making my way to the left and circling back in the direction of our home tent. I carefully creep across the site, my head on a swivel as I keep an eye on my surroundings.

A whistle from my left has me spinning in that direction, but then another whistle from my right has me drifting toward the home tent in a slow circle.

"Hey Defector," someone mutters in my ear before my body slips forward as the back of my head stings.

"What th–" I grunt as my face hits the muddy ground and my eyes roll into the back of my head.

I'm cold. Freezing cold.

There's something digging into my back and my clothes are damp.

My eyes finally flutter open, and darkness instantly greets me. I lift my head and shiver as a cool breeze rushes over me.

"Don't move too fast, they must've hit you really hard," says a feminine voice.

"What?"

"I think you'll be a little groggy for a while. Had

to bandage your head up with the scraps the guards gave me."

"Where am I?"

"Bordova. Dungeons probably."

Dungeons. Bordova.

Everything slowly starts to flash in my mind.

Leaving the task force tent.

Hearing someone outside.

The whistle that drew my attention.

I should've called out to someone; I should've left the tent with Alex and the rest of the team. I should've anticipated an attack to take place in the middle of the camp. I should've expected them to come for me.

"It all comin' back now?"

I nod and sit up further. "Who are you?"

The feminine voice laughs. "They hit you good then. What's your name?"

I think for a second. "Jake. Jake M something."

She giggles. "Well, it's nice to meet you Jake M Something. I'm Sara."

"My head hurts. A lot."

"It will. They hit you with something solid. I'm

actually surprised that it didn't kill you."

"Feels like it should've. It hurts a lot."

"Okay, you're going in circles now."

Metal bangs against metal, making us both jump.

"*Attecionsa*. Stand to attention please," a man bellows as he walks in front of our cell.

Sara helps me up, supporting me as we step toward the metal bars.

"I am Commander Ray Lotti, and I will be looking after you during your stay."

"Does that mean we'll be let go at the end?" A voice, from a few cells over, questions.

The Commander laughs, and through the dimness of the hallway, I can just about see him doubling over. "You stupid boy. This is your full circle moment. You are the children, and the grandchildren of the Defectors and your day of reckoning is here. Two hundred of you have been taken, and two hundred betrayed us many years ago. This is what you were meant for. *This* is your destiny."

"And what destiny would that be?" another prisoner asks.

"To pay for the sins of your elders, of course,"

Lotti says enthusiastically.

A series of murmurs and gasps echoes through the dungeon.

"So no, you won't be released. You will be buried in your final resting place opposite the House. A plot has been made for all of you, your name, your Defectors family member's name, and the day of your death. You will be immortalised as, not only symbols, but warnings." Lotti pauses. "Get some rest, we have a busy day ahead of us tomorrow."

CHAPTER EIGHT

Commander Lotti wakes us up at, what he claims to be, five in the morning.

We are given bottle green jumpsuits to put on before we're made to line up against the wall opposite our cells. Each of us receives a pair of handcuffs. They restrain our hands in front of us and put a connecting chain between us.

They guide us through the dungeon, up the stairs and through the House. We walk down the front steps of the House before we're separated from our connecting chain. The guards herd us into small groups. They then tell us to climb into the open topped carriages and sit quietly.

The carriages jolt into motion as they begin a convoy. They drive us through the streets of Bordova, the hot sun beating down on us. I count the streets as we go, so far we've passed through six. People emerge from their homes and watch as we pass by. They line both sides of the streets, all of them are cheering and shouting at us in Bordovan. My Bordovan is pretty good, but they're shouting so many different phrases all at the same time that I can't make out a single word.

We take a final left turn before our carriage slowly rolls to a stop. The pavements of this street are just as thickly lined with curious onlookers as the others were. They continue shouting though, matching the volume of those we've already passed, but they are quickly silenced as Commander Lotti stands atop the roof of his carriage.

"Citizens of Bordova, three years ago I promised to deliver those who wronged us just over seventy years ago, and today I am pleased to present to you those who will pay for their ancestors' transgressions. They will be publicly punished in the House's courtyard in three days. We encourage you to join us in the celebrations that will be hosted afterwards."

Everyone in the crowd cheers and screams in

support of Lotti's words. I look down at my feet as an unsavoury taste settles in my mouth. *Publicly punished.* A public punishment might entail humiliation, but my brain instantly shoots it down as it seems far to tame for Bordova.

"What do you think they'll do to us?" Sara whispers.

"I don't want to think about it," I respond.

"But you've thought about it, haven't you?"

I nod. "I'm trying not to, though. Don't want to give Lotti the satisfaction of seeing my fear."

Sara nods and turns back to look at Lotti.

"This is a triumphant time for our country. So come and rejoice with us as we punish the descendants of those who wronged us," he finishes. He waits a beat before hopping down from the top of his carriage. He gets back inside his carriage, and I hear him yell out an order to his driver.

The carriages start moving again and that's when I hear it. My name is being yelled from somewhere close. I twist around in my seat and that's when I lock eyes with Ilana.

Thea told her. Thea did what I asked her over two

years ago now.

"That's my girl," I mutter.

She's shouting my name as she tries to push through the crowd. So do a few others behind her, they all try to get through, but the sway of the crowd is too much. It keeps them pinned against the *Skull and Bone*.

"Ilana," I shout back, waving my cuffed hands at her as the carriage convoy starts to turn right at the top of the road.

As our carriage rounds the corner and Ilana slips out of my view.

CHAPTER NINE

The carriages don't stop again, instead they take us right back to the House. We're helped down from our carriages before being guided back to our cells.

For a moment I don't think they're going to take our cuffs off, but thankfully, they do. They also give us each a small tray of food to consume, a tray I hear the guards laughing about, calling it our final, proper meal.

And it does turn out to be our final proper meal, but not in the sense that it's the last thing we'll eat, because the three days before the public punishment pass by far too quickly for my liking. We're given three breakfasts, each one the same tiny bowl of sticky, flavourless oats. Three lunches which consist of two pieces of slightly stale bread with funny tasting butter that I think is out of date by at least a week. And then three dinners of overly steamed vegetables, in an odd tasting broth. I can't really complain since they're keeping us fed and watered which wasn't something I thought would happen.

On the morning of our punishment, we're woken up early and forced into the showers. We're given five minutes to wash ourselves and get out. The water is freezing cold, and the water pressure is hard which makes the droplets feel like tiny rocks bouncing off of my skin.

"Five minutes is up. Get out and move along," the guard, who is monitoring our showers, yells.

Everyone in the showers exits their cubicles and grabs the ratty, threadbare towels that were given to us beforehand. We all form an orderly line, our towels wrapped around our waists or torsos. The guard quickly does a walk by to make sure that everyone has joined the line before we're escorted back to our cells.

"You worried at all?" Sara asks as I walk back into the cell and a guard shuts the door behind me.

I shrug. "It's not ideal, but we're going to be okay."

"Is that something you really believe?" she asks with disgust, as though the prospect of thinking of a better outcome is the vilest thing she's ever heard of.

"I don't know. I'm holding out hope because a precaution I took a few years ago seems to have reached the people it was meant to. I'm holding onto that little bit of hope, but it's not a lifeline. Anything could happen today and I'm not naive to that," I explain to her as I change.

She nods and sighs. We fall into a pleasant, but strained silence as we lay on our respective beds. I know that she's thinking about what might happen today, I've been thinking about it too. But I'm praying that my small amount of hope is going to be something I can depend on, something I can cling to even when the worst thing is happening to us. We've no idea what awaits us outside of these cells and that is scary. A ball of tension forms in my stomach at the thought of what is awaiting us.

"*Attecionsa*. Stand to attention please," Commander Lotti shouts as he walks past the cells. "One by one your cells will be opened, and you will be cuffed and chained to the line."

We listen as the three cells before us are opened and the prisoners are chained up. When it comes to our turn, I exit first and present my wrists to the guards. They aggressively slap the cuffs on my wrists before attaching my wrists to the connecting chain. Then it's Sara's turn and once the guard has moved on, I carefully turn and check on her.

"You doing okay?"

"I think so. Sorry for snappin' earlier, I think I'm finally losin' it."

"Don't worry abou–" I get cut off by my head snapping to the right. My cheek burns and when I look up Commander Lotti is standing in front of me, his hand poised from the slap he just delivered.

"No talking. This isn't a social event. Turn back around, or the next one won't be a slap," he threatens, which has me turning back around quickly.

We begin shuffling out of the dungeon corridor, up the stairs. The guards and Lotti walk us through the House until we come to a little corridor in which the sky can be seen. It feels like years since I've seen the sky, and while the hope that has settled inside of me has kept me feeling pessimistic about our chances of survival, the niggling feeling resettles at the back of my mind and I begin to fear that Ilana and her team won't reach me in time.

"Out there is the arena. Droves of people have gathered to witness today's festivities, so please, try and conduct yourselves with some kind of decorum," Lotti explains.

The guards start to guide us forward and as we emerge into the sunlight we all groan, our eyes squinting shut. The rays of the sun burn our eyes as they begin to adjust as Lotti has us parade around the arena like show animals, walking us in a circle as the crowd claps and boos.

As the guards guide us back toward the tunnel, I catch sight of a crowd member that I saw at the parade. The girl who was standing next to Ilana when I was calling out to her. She looks worried and when she looks down at me, I can see the pitying look on her face. *She knows what's about to happen.*

Back in the tunnel, we turn around in the tight space and reform the line we started in. There's a slight pause in all the action. The audience has gone quiet as well and I crane my neck to try and see what's going on. I do that until three guards come along and undo the chains of the six people in front of me, my own chains and Sara's as well. They guide the eight of us out of the tunnel and back into the arena.

"Now let us begin the celebrations," says the announcer as the eight of us are guided over to the newly erected wooden posts.

I have a vague idea of what's about to happen and I hang my head as a guard comes along and raises my hands above my head. He loops a rope that is dangling from the top of the wooden post through the connecting chain of the cuffs before briefly walking away.

CHAPTER TEN

I'm numb. My whole body feels weightless as I stare at the sandy floor of the arena. I feel sick as well, nausea rolling over me in waves.

This is it, this is our punishment. This is the final time we'll see the sun, the beautiful blue sky which really should be cloudy to represent how we are feeling. To represent the sadness and mourning that is going to come from our deaths.

When Lotti said we were going to be *buried in your final resting place opposite the House,* I knew what was going to happen. We all did. We weren't naive to the outcome of our stay in the dungeons, but I was naive to let the hope that came with seeing Ilana build a home inside of me. I shouldn't have let myself prepare for Ilana and her friends to save me. I shouldn't let those thoughts of a rescue get to my head.

I look up at the crowd one last time. I glance through the crowd and look for the girl from the parade. I find her easily; she's standing with a group of boys right at the back of the first circle. They all look apprehensive, worried. The announcer starts speaking again but I don't listen because all I can focus on is them. Then Ilana appears. She pushes through the crowd until she reaches the group. They have a brief conversation before she turns and sees me tied to the wooden post. She screams what I believe to be my name, but the sound is swallowed by the cheers of the crowd. Her shouts ease as her facial expression morphs into one of fear. We make eye contact one last time before I force myself to look away.

I focus my gaze on the arena in front of me and see members of the Bordovan Military lining up in front of us. Rifles are slung over their shoulders as they take up positions opposite us. The guards who were patrolling our cells come and stand in front of us. The one in front of me lifts his hands and I see a strip of black fabric. *A blindfold*, I deduce as I take a deep breath.

I quickly look back up at Ilana, wanting her to be the last thing I see. A part of me feels guilty, if I could see anyone in my final moments, I'd want it to be Thea, but she's not here and for that I am glad. I wouldn't want her to see this. I want her memories of me to be positive, to be of the times we spent together, not of me dying.

I come back to the arena in front of me and as the guard raises the blindfold to my eyes, I catch sight of Ilana being held back by one of the men behind her. She's crying and seems to be yelling at him, but her yelling quickly turns into begging as my vision becomes obscured.

Time slows down the second the guard finishes tying the blindfold. I can hear the crowd screaming, cheering as the announcer begins a countdown.

Three...

Two..

One.

My body jolts and only a brief amount of pain radiates from the left side of my chest before my feet give way. I fall forwards and my cuffs are the only thing keeping my body upright. I blink a few times against the fabric, and I feel it get damp from the few tears that escape my eyes before nothingness takes over.

I become light and floaty. My body goes first. Then my heart slows all the way down and I can feel every single beat. It feels like a countdown, one beat, two beat, three beat, four beat and the final beat.

The final beat feels drawn out before my heart stops beating completely, and I give in to the darkness.

Language Glossary

<u>Bordovan</u>

Ey, mi li'tet sakcho – Hello, my little boy

Mia srolto, reba yael mi toullo romazitca ilo Jake arsh dianquo orow pari anniversitaro – My daughter, you must tell me all the romantic things Jake has done for your anniversary.

Mi sakcho – My boy

Attecionsa – Attention

ABOUT THE AUTHOR

A. Carys is a self-published author from Portsmouth, United Kingdom. Other than spending 90% of her day writing, she also loves to crochet, read, and take photos of her family's cats.

Printed in Great Britain
by Amazon

42362080R00040